# ANIMAL LIVES

MARGARET LANE is a naturalist and author of the biography of Beatrix Potter. In this new series, she combines her knowledge of wildlife with her understanding of children. Do all squirrels hibernate? Are they shy? The answers to many questions are presented in a realistic story that will intrigue young imaginations. Detailed and superbly naturalistic illustrations make this book a perfect introduction to the life of squirrels.

Additional title: THE FROG

To Octavius M.L.

To Kathy K.L.

First published in Great Britain 1981
by Methuen Children's Books Ltd
First published in Picture Lions 1983
by William Collins Sons & Co Ltd
8 Grafton Street, London W1

Printed in Great Britain
by William Collins Sons & Co Ltd, Glasgow

# THE SQUIRREL

By Margaret Lane

Illustrations by
Kenneth Lilly

FONTANA
PICTURE LIONS

A squirrel scampers through the treetops as safely as if he were on a garden path. He is the acrobat and tight-rope walker of the woods. He runs along branches, holding on to twigs with his long fingers, swinging from tree to tree, going up or down their trunks as easily as a fly. He hangs happily upside down on the trunk of a tree, enjoying the spring sun, or sits upright to eat his food, holding it in his hands.

The red squirrel is a very handsome fellow. His coat is reddish-brown with creamy-white belly. His bushy tail, which helps him to balance in the treetops, curls up his back like a question-mark when he sits upright. In summer he has long tufts of hair on the tips of his ears, almost like tassels, but these disappear in the autumn moult. In winter his furry tail becomes almost white.

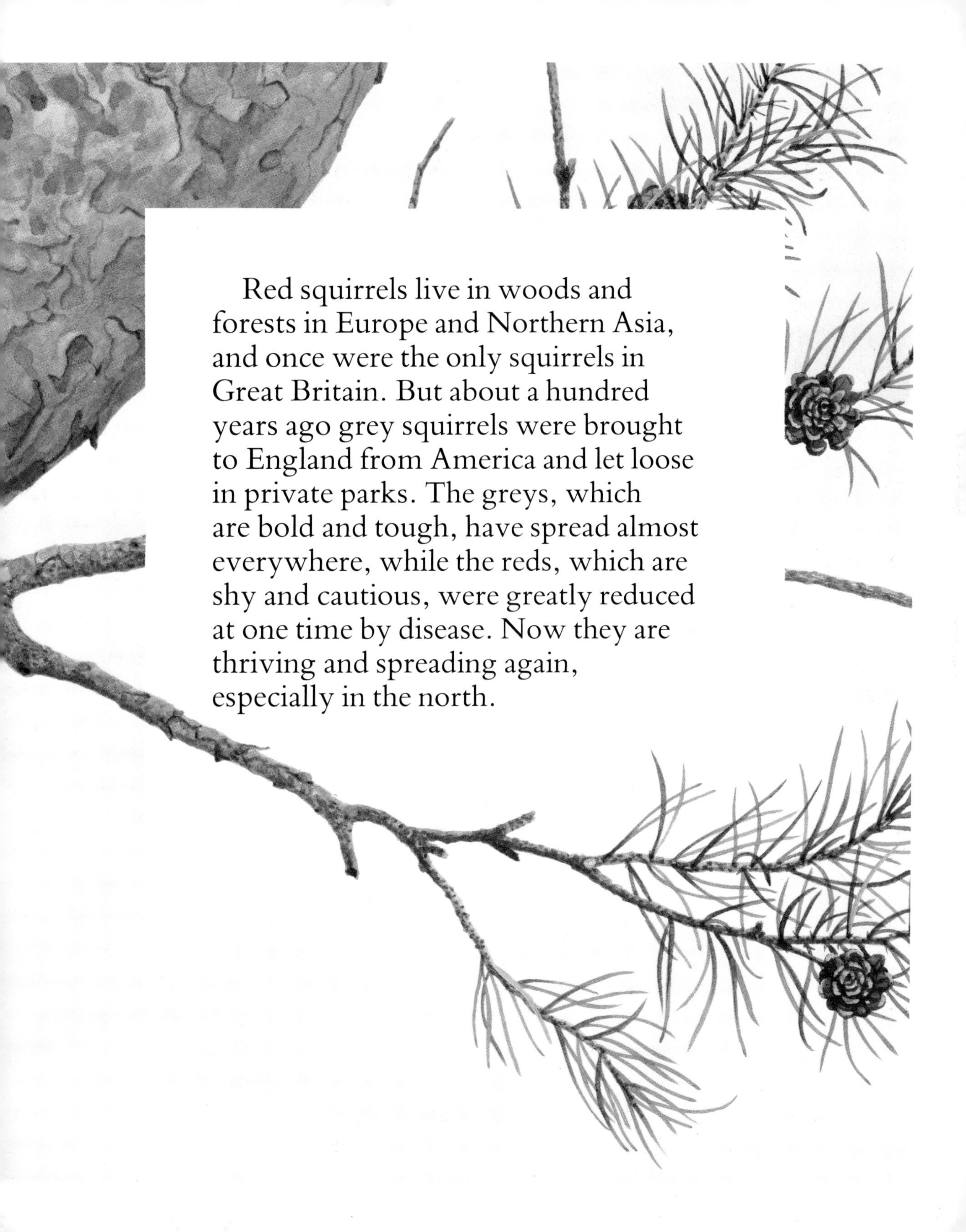

Red squirrels live in woods and forests in Europe and Northern Asia, and once were the only squirrels in Great Britain. But about a hundred years ago grey squirrels were brought to England from America and let loose in private parks. The greys, which are bold and tough, have spread almost everywhere, while the reds, which are shy and cautious, were greatly reduced at one time by disease. Now they are thriving and spreading again, especially in the north.

The red and grey squirrel like different kinds of woods. The reds are happiest among pines and conifers, since their favourite food is the seed they find in fir cones. They hold the cones in their hands and strip them with their long sharp teeth. They also like nuts and acorns, berries and toadstools, and when food is plentiful make little holes in the ground and bury their nuts. Each squirrel keeps to his own part of the wood, so he may just find them again if he is lucky.

Grey squirrels, on the other hand, prefer mixed woods of oak, ash, beech and hazel, where there are plenty of beechnuts and acorns in autumn, hips and haws in the hedges, leaf buds and juicy stems at most times of the year. They will also strip bark from a tree to get at the sap beneath. This can damage the tree and makes them unpopular with foresters, who shoot them when they can. The grey squirrel is also fond of birds' eggs and will steal them from the nest or even run off with the nestlings. And he is not above digging up crocus bulbs in your garden.

Both the red and the grey squirrel are clever builders. They make themselves nests, called dreys, high up in the trees, where they are safe from most enemies. The balloon-shaped nest, made of leaves, twigs, grass and strips of tree bark, is built among the branches. It has no door, but is so soft and loose that the squirrel can always push his way in or out. Before the birth of her babies a mother squirrel plucks soft fur from her belly to line the nest, so that the little ones will be warm in a soft bed.

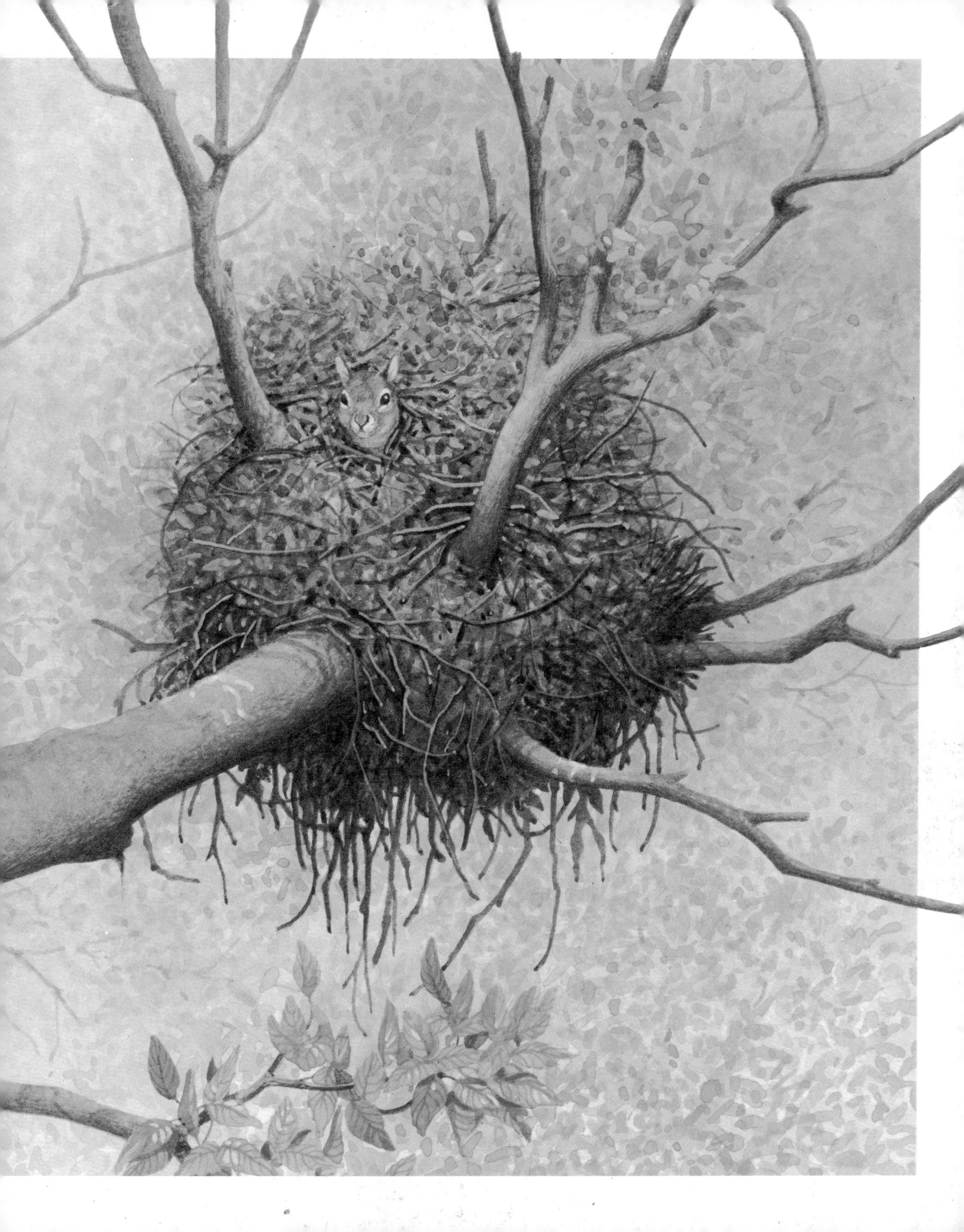

Squirrels choose their mates in early spring, the male chasing off any rivals who come near. When he sees another male he squeaks, chatters and whines, flicking his bushy tail and rushing about in the branches to scare off the stranger. If a female appears he fluffs up his tail and chatters and dances around her. They mate without wasting time and set about preparing their nest in the high branches. It will soon be hidden in a screen of green leaves. The baby squirrels, called 'kittens', will be born in about six weeks.

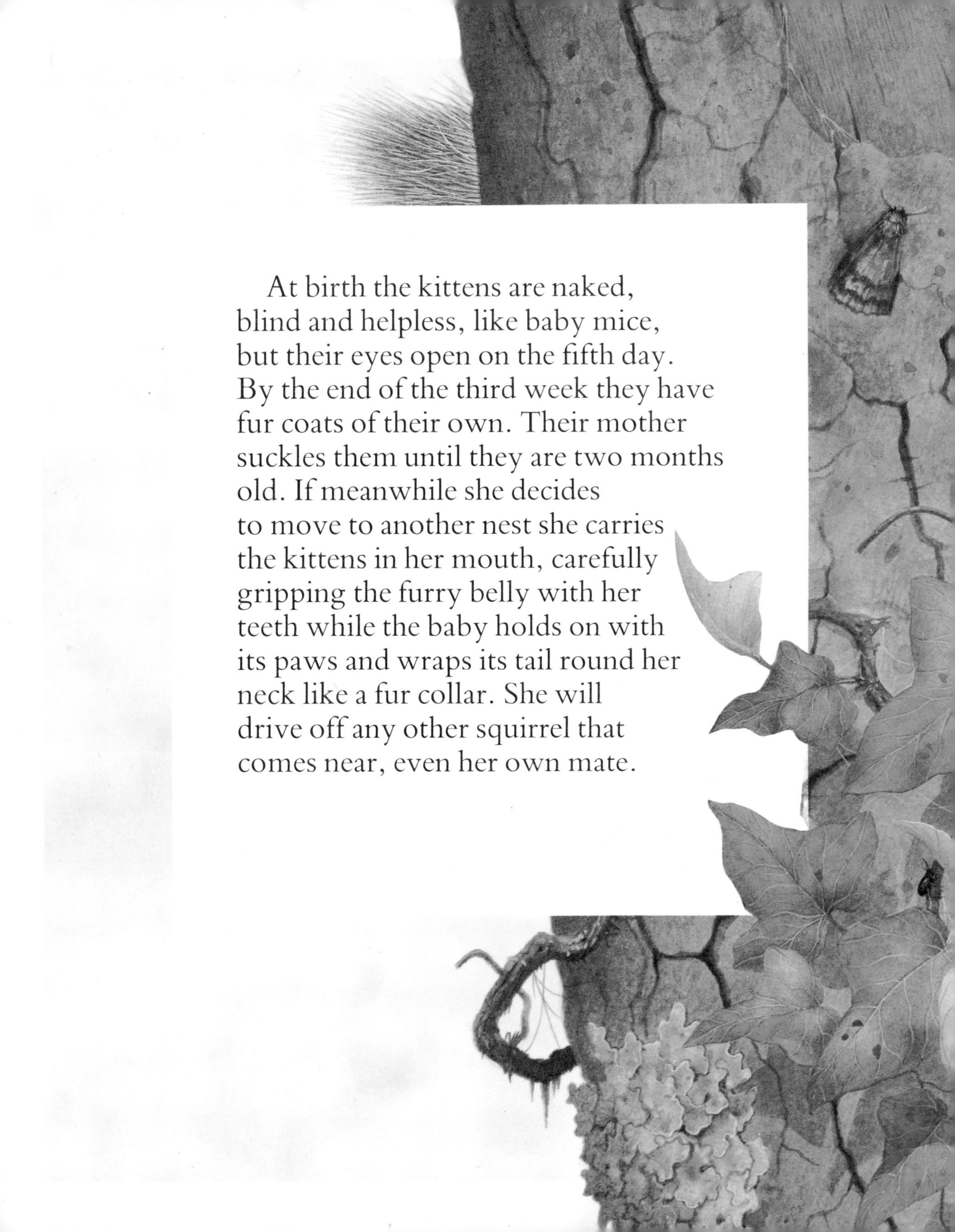

At birth the kittens are naked, blind and helpless, like baby mice, but their eyes open on the fifth day. By the end of the third week they have fur coats of their own. Their mother suckles them until they are two months old. If meanwhile she decides to move to another nest she carries the kittens in her mouth, carefully gripping the furry belly with her teeth while the baby holds on with its paws and wraps its tail round her neck like a fur collar. She will drive off any other squirrel that comes near, even her own mate.

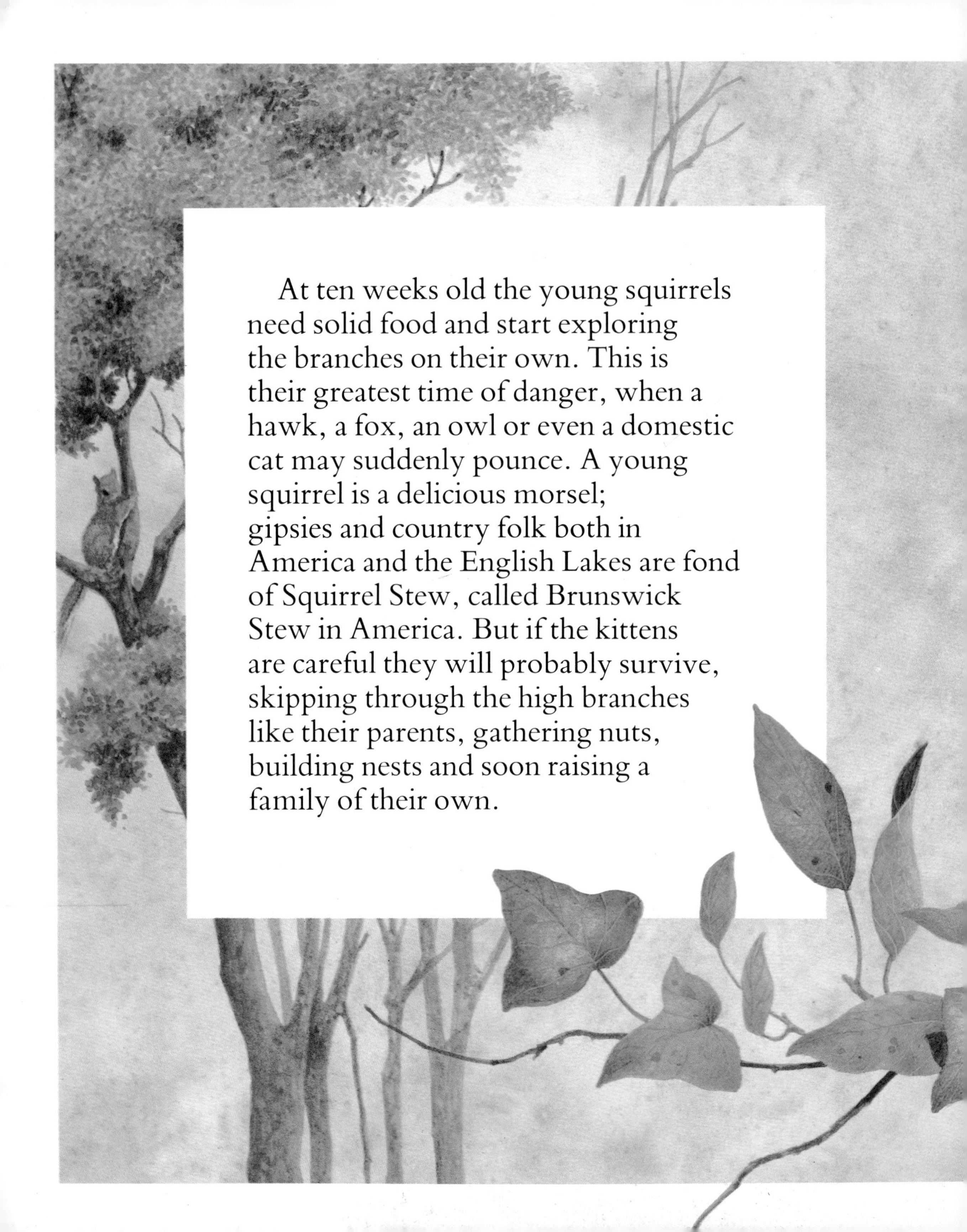

At ten weeks old the young squirrels need solid food and start exploring the branches on their own. This is their greatest time of danger, when a hawk, a fox, an owl or even a domestic cat may suddenly pounce. A young squirrel is a delicious morsel; gipsies and country folk both in America and the English Lakes are fond of Squirrel Stew, called Brunswick Stew in America. But if the kittens are careful they will probably survive, skipping through the high branches like their parents, gathering nuts, building nests and soon raising a family of their own.

Many people believe that squirrels sleep all winter in their nests, but this is not true. In very cold weather they may stay in bed for two or three days, keeping warm, but they soon become hungry and come down their tree to hunt for food, even in the snow. At such times they search for nuts and scraps that they have buried. If they live near houses the grey squirrel, hungry and bold, will raid bird-tables. The shy red squirrel is not easily seen in winter in the dark fir woods, but he is awake all the same. He lives off what he can find, or on fir-cones and nuts stored in a hollow tree

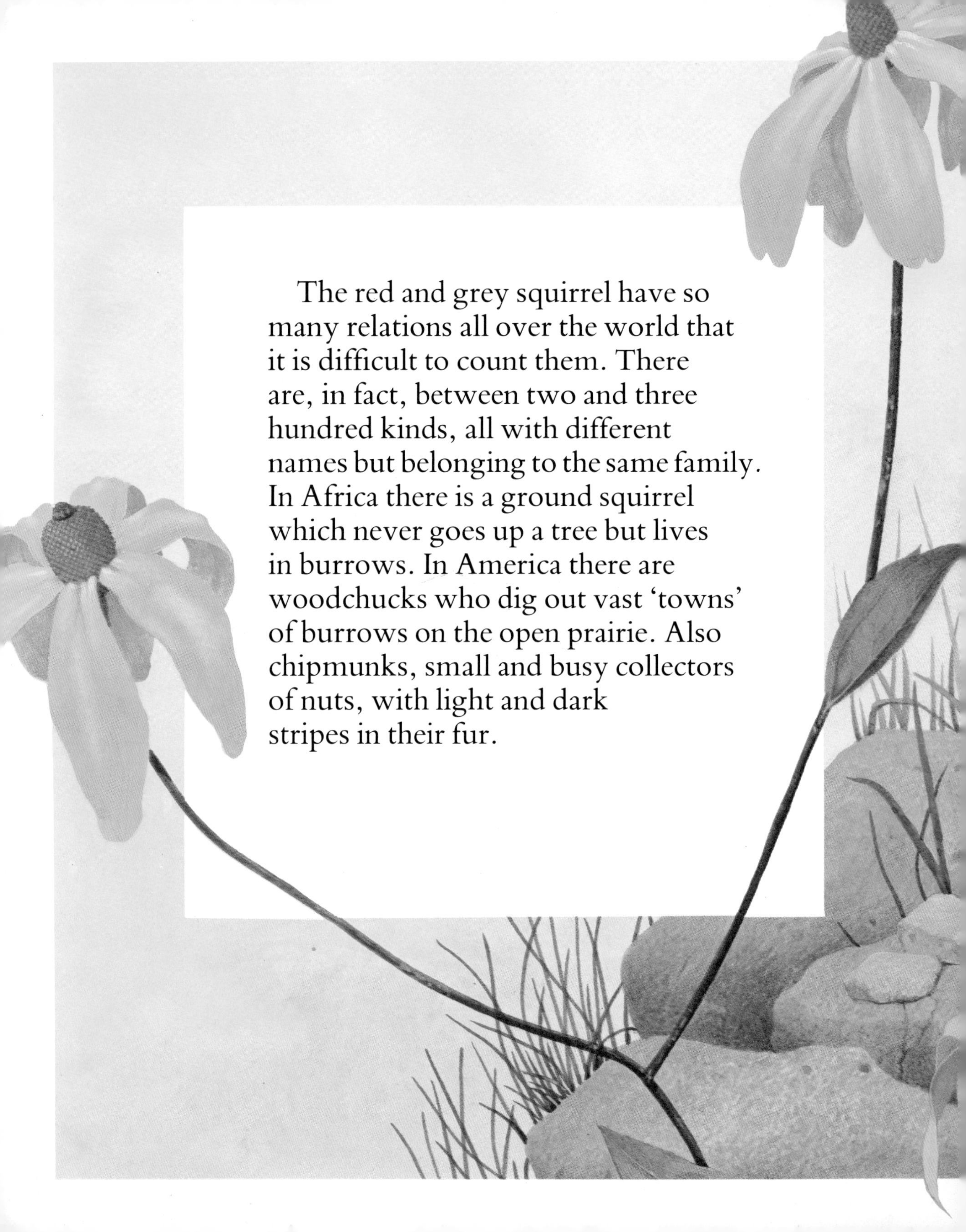

The red and grey squirrel have so many relations all over the world that it is difficult to count them. There are, in fact, between two and three hundred kinds, all with different names but belonging to the same family. In Africa there is a ground squirrel which never goes up a tree but lives in burrows. In America there are woodchucks who dig out vast 'towns' of burrows on the open prairie. Also chipmunks, small and busy collectors of nuts, with light and dark stripes in their fur.

Many of these relations, unlike the red and the grey squirrel, *do* sleep all winter, having got very fat in autumn and waking up thin and hungry in the spring. And there are many flying squirrels too, both in the north and in the tropics. They perform wonderful gliding leaps from tree to tree by means of a loose fold of skin which spreads out like a rug when they jump and carries them great distances through the air. Wherever they live, squirrels are quick, clever and agile creatures, making the best of things wherever they happen to be, in woods, forests, mountains, deserts, parks and suburbs.